More
Parts

Tedd Arnold

SCHOLASTIC INC.

New York   Toronto   London   Auckland   Sydney
Mexico City   New Delhi   Hong Kong   Buenos Aires

To Mom and Dad—

There are still some things
I'd like explained.

ISBN 0-439-51977-2

Copyright © 2001 by Tedd Arnold. All rights reserved. Published by Scholastic Inc.,
557 Broadway, New York, NY 10012, by arrangement with Dial Books for Young
Readers, a member of Penguin Putnam Inc. SCHOLASTIC and associated logos are
trademarks and/or registered trademarks of Scholastic Inc.

12 11 10 9 8 7 6 5 4 3 2   3 4 5 6 7 8/0

Printed in the U.S.A.   09

First Scholastic printing, February 2003

Typography by Nancy R. Leo-Kelly

This art was prepared using color pencils and watercolor washes,
and the text was hand-lettered by Mr. Arnold.

Things are bad — and getting worse!
Each day it's something new.
With all the stuff I hear about
I don't know what to do.

One day I tripped on my red truck
And it just fell apart.
But when I told my mom, she said,
"I'll bet that broke your heart."

I guess that's possible. Who knows?
I don't think Mom would lie.
I'd better play more carefully.
This pillow's worth a try.

People say all kinds of things
That I don't understand.
Like when my dad asked me if I
Would please give him a hand.

I didn't know my hands come off,
And I don't want them to!
So I'll make sure that they stay on
With gloves and lots of glue.

Our next-door neighbor had a joke
He wanted us to hear.
He said, "It's sure to crack you up!"
I ran away in fear.

Who wants to hear a joke like that?
Not my idea of fun!
I gotta keep my head together.
It's my only one.

My teacher has me worried too.
This happened yesterday:
She said to stretch our arms and legs
Before we go and play.

I'm sure she thinks it's good for us,
But that's just too bizarre!
My arms and legs are long enough.
I like the way they are.

I know I've got a lot to learn.
I'm little and I'm young.
But what did Grandma really mean
When she said, "Hold your tongue"?

My tongue's a slimy, jiggly, squishy,
Slippery little squirt.
It'd be my luck to squeeze too hard
And lose it in the dirt.

So I decided that it's best
  To stay here in my room.
'Cause who knows when some little thing
  Just might lead to my

DOOM?

Then Mom and Dad came in and asked me,
"Why are you upset?"

I told them all the things I've heard
That get me in a sweat.

Like Coach, who says before each game
Is ready to begin,
He gets so nervous that he nearly
Jumps out of his skin.

Or what a friend said recently—
It gave me such a fright!
He claimed his baby sister screams
Her lungs out every night.

My skin could slip, my head may crack,
And I might break my heart.
I could lose my lungs, my hands—
Who knows when it might start?
What if quite by accident
My body flies apart?

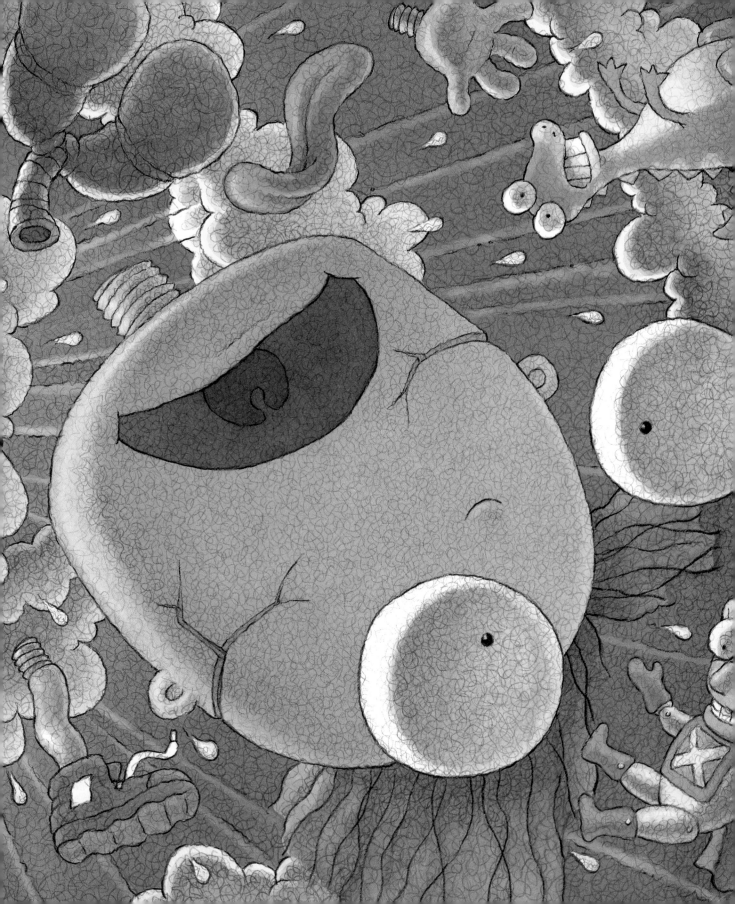

Mom and Dad just smiled and looked
Relieved that I'm okay.
And Mom explained to me about
The things that people say.

And though Dad laughed, I know he didn't
Mean to be unkind
When he said, "For a minute, son . . .